We Read
PHONICS™

Robot Man

TREASURE BAY

Parent's Introduction

Welcome to **We Read Phonics**! This series is designed to help you assist your child in reading. Each book includes a story, as well as some simple word games to play with your child. The games focus on the phonics skills and sight words your child will use in reading the story.

Here are some recommendations for using this book with your child:

1 Word Play

There are word games both before and after the story. Make these games fun and playful. If your child becomes bored or frustrated, play a different game or take a break.

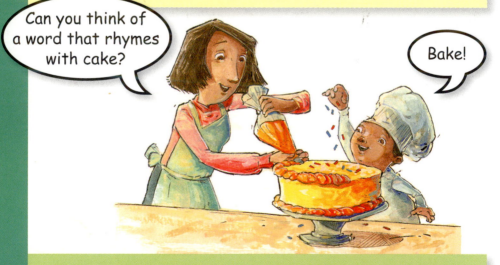

Can you think of a word that rhymes with cake?

Bake!

Phonics is a method of sounding out words by blending together letter sounds. However, not all words can be "sounded out." **Sight words** are frequently used words that usually cannot be sounded out.

2 Read the Story

After some word play, read the story aloud to your child—or read the story together, by reading aloud at the same time or by taking turns. As you and your child read, move your finger under the words.

Next, have your child read the entire story to you while you follow along with your finger under the words. If there is some difficulty with a word, either help your child to sound it out or wait about five seconds and then say the word.

3 Discuss and Read Again

After reading the story, talk about it with your child. Ask questions like, "What happened in the story?" and "What was the best part?" It will be helpful for your child to read this story to you several times. Another great way for your child to practice is by reading the book to a younger sibling, a pet, or even a stuffed animal!

This time, let's read the story together!

LEVEL 4 Level 4 introduces words with long "e," "o," and "u" (as in *Pete, nose,* and *flute*) and the long "e" sound made with the vowel pairs "ee" and "ea." It also introduces the soft "c" and "g" sounds (as in *nice* and *cage*), and "or" (as in *sports*).

Robot Man

A We Read Phonics™ Book
Level 4

Text Copyright © 2010 by Treasure Bay, Inc.
Illustrations Copyright © 2010 by Jeffrey Ebbeler

Reading Consultants: Bruce Johnson, M.Ed., and Dorothy Taguchi, Ph.D.

We Read Phonics™ is a trademark of Treasure Bay, Inc.

Published by
Treasure Bay, Inc.
P.O. Box 119
Novato, CA 94948 USA

Printed in Singapore

Library of Congress Catalog Card Number: 2010921691

Hardcover ISBN: 978-1-60115-329-6
Paperback ISBN: 978-1-60115-330-2

We Read Phonics™
Patent Pending

Visit us online at:
www.TreasureBayBooks.com

PR 07/10

Robot Man

By Paul Orshoski

Illustrated by Jeffrey Ebbeler

Phonics Game

Alphabet Soup

Creating words using certain letters will help your child read this story.

Materials: thick paper or cardboard; scissors; pencils, crayons, or markers; small cooking pot and stirring spoon

1. Cut 40 two x two inch squares from the paper or cardboard and print letter and letter combinations on the squares. Make two each with r, b, t, m, n, ea, ee, w, d, s, c, l, p, u, and c. Make three cards with "a" and "e." Make four cards with "o."

2. Place the letters into a pretend pot of soup and stir the pot! Then, players take turns taking letters from the pot. When a player can make a word by putting his letters together, he makes and reads the word out loud. Once a word is made, the player can use the letters in that word (and other letters) to make new words. If scoring, give a point for each word that is made.

3. Players take turns taking letters and making new words. Once a player has nine letters, he must put one letter back in the pot in order to take another letter.

4. If scoring, the words *robot* and *man* can be bonus words worth an extra point. If a player can make both *robot* and *man* at the same time, he automatically wins!

5. The winner is the first player to score 12 points. Then, put all the letters back into the pretend pot of soup and play again!

Some words that can be made with these letters include *weeds, clean, made, space, speed, cream,* and *sweet.*

Memory

This is a fun way to practice recognizing some sight words used in the story.

1. Write each word listed on the right on two plain 3 x 5 inch cards, so you have two sets of cards. Using one set of cards, ask your child to repeat each word after you. Shuffle both decks of cards together, and place them face down on a flat surface.

2. The first player turns over one card and says the word, then turns over a second card and says the word. If the cards match, the player takes those cards and continues to play. If they don't match, both cards are turned over, and it's the next player's turn.

3. Keep the cards. You can make more cards with other **We Read Phonics** books and combine the cards for even bigger games!

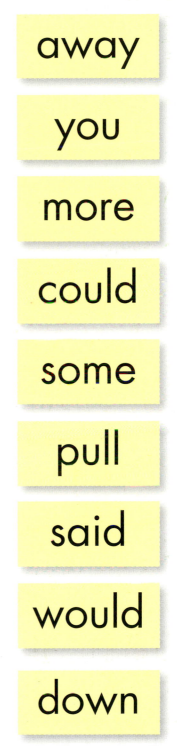

away

you

more

could

some

pull

said

would

down

Pull the weeds and clean the sink.

Toss the trash away. It stinks!

These are jobs my dad must do.

And Mom said I must do them too.

So Dad and I made up a plan . . .

. . . to make a space-age robot man.

The robot man came in a kit.

Too bad not all the parts would fit.

Dad got the robot man to go.

He made the robot wave hello.

The robot man did all the jobs.

So Dad and I could sit like blobs.

The robot man would hoe and weed.

He drove me home at quite a speed.

He froze us all some ice cream treats.

I have to tell you, life was sweet!

Yes, life was good, and all was swell.
Then robot man went plunk and fell.

The robot man was out of whack.
He put the ice cream down my back.

Those brand new lamps,
I will not miss.

But then from Mom
he stole a kiss.

My mom said there was no excuse.
And robot man had no more use.

So Mom sent us to hit the sack.
And then she sent the robot back.

Phonics Game

Word Cross

Creating words from these letters will help your child practice building words like those in this story.

Materials: Use the same letter cards created for Alphabet Soup (see page 2).

1. Place the cards with the letter side down on a table. Each player draws five cards.

2. The first player tries to make a word using the cards. If no word can be made, the player discards one card and draws another card, and it becomes the next player's turn.

3. If the first player can make a word using the cards, the player makes the word going across. After making a word, a player receives one point for each letter used and draws enough cards to maintain five cards.

4. Subsequent words must be built upon words previously made, either across or down, in a crossword pattern. For example, if the first player builds the word *red,* then the next player must build a word going down, using "r," "e," or "d," such as *seed* or *rude.*

5. Consider playing with both players showing their letters and helping each other.

Phonics Game

Rhyming

Practicing rhyming words helps children learn how words are similar.

What rhymes with treat?

Sweet!

1 Explain to your child that these words rhyme because they have the same end sounds: *sink, stink, link, mink, pink, rink, think,* and *wink.*

2 Ask your child to say a word that rhymes with *sink.*

3 If your child has trouble, offer some possible answers or repeat step 1. It's okay to accept nonsense words, for example, *bink.*

4 When your child is successful, repeat step 2 with these words:

plan (possible answers: *can, Dan, fan, man, pan, ran, tan, van*)

kit (possible answers: *bit, fit, hit, lit, mitt, knit, pit, sit, wit*)

jobs (possible answers: *blobs, Bobs, globs, lobs, mobs, sobs*)

weed (possible answers: *bead, seed, deed, feed, heed, lead, need, read*)

treat (possible answers: *beat, feet, heat, meet, neat, seat, sweet, wheat*)

whack (possible answers: *back, hack, Jack, knack, pack, rack, sack, tack*)

If you liked **Robot Man,**
here is another **We Read Phonics** book you are sure to enjoy!

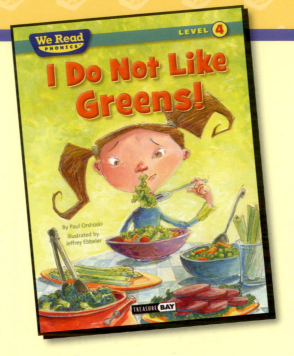

I Do Not Like Greens!

Greens, greens, and more greens! Dad likes to cook, but he will only cook healthy food. What if you want some sweet and fatty junk food? Well, junk food is okay—if you are Dad's dog. But for his little girl, Dad only serves greens and other foods that are good for her. What's a girl to do?